Praise for Erin Little

"I am thinking about longing, the oldest poetic concept, and the ways in which Erin Little brings longing to an unmatched understanding, one that is crucial, painful, and innermost in her debut chapbook, *Personal Injury*. Little is a writer I would follow anywhere. Her interrogations of longing take us through multiple and immediate dimensions: longing through the body as a cancer patient in a hospital; longing through her parents praying for a complete cure; longing as a youth in pain needing to be heard; and longing as an adult feeling love in rain and the rain in love. She implores the reader to be thoughtful with their words—this move hits the highest poetic marks. Little questions the definition of love, and she makes me stop—I turn the corner and this meditation will forever unwind in me."

—Dorothy Chan, author of *Babe* and *Return of the Chinese Femme*

"Understanding since childhood that death can come from within, the speaker of these poems is acutely conscious of the various and particular ways her body remains present in the world, as a lover, daughter, observer, friend. Erin Little sets these experiences down with assuredness, even when they hurt. These poems record something akin to what Rilke once described as 'the chill, uncertain sunlight of those long / childhood hours when you were so afraid,' but they also make room for a 'face lit like a bulb / ecstatic as a baby who's found some / thing that moves her.' There's cracks of light in the gloom, there's blood within a life. *Personal Injury* makes space for all of it, in gorgeous language and wonderfully sharp images. It's a joy to read this work."

—Heather Christle, author of *The Crying Book* and *Heliopause*

"Erin Little's *Personal Injury* plays with physical harm and emotional hurt as it plays with poetic structures—from the sonnet and the villanelle to the list and the chart. Each poem tangles with its own existence and makes its reader question what existence is for, if not for relishing our entanglements."

—Mark Yakich, author of *Spiritual Exercises* and *The Importance Of Peeling Potatoes In Ukraine*

Personal Injury

Erin Little

Chestnut Review
Ithaca, New York
https://chestnutreview.com
ISBN: 9798866253531

Personal Injury

Erin Little

Chestnut Review Chapbooks

Contents

I

II

III

For Lynne, John, and Kelly Little

I

Elegy

for Leah

I used to live on a hospital wing
in a terrible white bed. I made
a friend, a girl my age.
Sandy blonde once
upon a time spent playing
dress-up in the rec room, laughing
at things long since slipped
from memory.

To recover personal history
lost   to the shrapnel of grief,
I become the bed, giant terrible white we
trusted them. Clean structure who cradled
her body, felt a chorus of tiny joints giving
in. I never saw her, dead in the starched
mouth. But I imagine a doll
smothered in the jaw of a white whale.

Diagnosis

Sit
on the exam table,
crinkle the paper
with your weight.

Sink
through your shoulders
when the man in white
opens the door.

Search
the room for Mom
while the man searches
your flesh with cold hands.

Do
the deep breaths when
he asks for them.
He says he is from   *on-call-o-gee.*

But we are from Dallas and *where*   *is*
that?

                                                        a place to be from?

                        where is? Mom?

Hear
pen scratch   against clipboard,
watch his lips   make   the shape

                                        of bad news.

To the ███████ Parents:

October 1999

███████████

███████ you may ██████ know ███████████

███████ our daughter ████ has acute lymphoblastic leukemia

██████████████████████ we want ██

██

██

███████████████████████████████████ a complete

cure. ███████████████████████████ early █

████████████████ evidence ████████████████

her blood ██████ █ her █████ fluid.

███████████████████ chemotherapy ███ the next two and

one-half years ████████████████████████████

begun ██████ and will continue for ████████████

██

█████████ hope and expectation that █████ leukemia

will be █ remiss █████████████ she ███████████

six-month therapy █████████████████ two-year main-

tenance ██████████████ the vast majority

of ██████████████████████████████████████

██████ Children ████████████████████████████

██ hope and expect ████████████████ to attend

school ███████████████████ and play with ███ friends.

███ therapy ████████████████████████ 's

ability to fight ████████████████

█████████████████████████████████████

█████████████████████████████████████

███████████████████████████████ is

fortunate ████████████████████████████

however, we understand █████████████████

████████████████████████████ she would

put other children ████████████ at risk. ████████

██████████████ avoid close contact with ██████

█████████████████████████████████████

█████████████████████████████████████

████████ a live virus (████████████████

█████████████████████████████████████

█████████████████████████████████████

█████████████████████████████████████

█████████████████████████████████████

████████ a fever, ███ or ████ infection ████████

█████████████████████████████████████

her doctors ████████████ do what they deem appropriate.

███████████████████ the ████████████ prayers we

█████████████████████████████████████

████████ will keep you ████████████████.

████████████████████

The Molting

I don't remember who was first to say it. That my head looked like a nest. Crown of twigs, haunting of scalp. It came out in swatches and hanks, frayed in the morning pillowcase. Watching *Arthur* in the living room, it came down a dry rain when I shifted my weight.

A six-year-old's pale gelatin head, how or whether to shave it. How weather hits a bare scalp. How metal teeth eat the evidence away. Better to clean hair off furniture, sheets, clothing, carpet. Better to molt over time. To cover the rotted feathers with a hat. Better, better, better, better, better.

Pain Scale

"The Wong-Baker FACES® Pain Rating Scale was created by Donna Wong and Connie Baker in 1983 to help children effectively communicate about their pain."

—*WongBakerFaces.org*

0

**No
Hurt**

this one is a lie

please believe me

2

**Hurts
Little Bit**

the pills—

slimy chalk lines left
on my tongue, pills down my gullet

sometimes mom needs to cut
the pills with the pill cutter

sometimes I hide the pieces
in the trashcan and tell no one

4

**Hurts
Little More**

blood pressure cuff's
embrace already too
tight, making hot stars

inside my arm why was I
always alone
in that room

6

**Hurts
Even More**

I move without knowing it—
the squishy tube constricts,
the stars in my arm boil and explode
but no one notices because
they haven't taken
the blood yet

the blood taker's name is Esther,
she pricks my finger warm
into tubes with different colored caps
sometimes the finger is not enough,
sometimes Esther needs more,
she needs to take more blood
from more places she doesn't mean
for it to hurt the way it does

8

**Hurts
Whole Lot**

sometimes I'm allowed to go home
for a while, sleep in my room
with giant windows the sun

loves to peak through, but when
the light pounds my head
I forget how to say—

burble white grape juice
until it fills the bed,
covers the covers

my parents tape top sheets
to the windows my parents
say maybe it's time to go back

10

**Hurts
Worst**

at home
in the laundry room
after a shower you twist
a towel backwards
onto my head, the sculpture
meant to dry hair, the sculpture
that lives on your head most days

it unfurls from me a moan a yelp a cry
the only time I remember asking you, mom,
if I would die

Whale Poem

Brace for the gun
-metal damp,
the day's malaise.

The doorway is
a pit and the stairs
feel ambitious.

A friend tells me
it matters that I break
up the day with sleep.

Skip the dull parts,
with their beatdown
iron taste, droopy edges.

The rain falls
bronze out there.
I don't envy it.

Beached whale
blanched ashore.
When the whale

dies it fells the
ocean down slowly,
over the course

of a day. The other
fish see it fall bit by
bit. Heavy with minutes

turned to hours.
Dozens of organisms
will move into the body

once it settles—a new
home to sustain them.
Safer inside than out.

II

O

Sunday	Monday	Tuesday	
	Dr Dan Bowers Andrea Windick, RN CLINIC: 214 456 2382		
3	4	5	6
10	11	12	13
17	18	19	20 IVA Spin Vinc Dex.
24 Devamethasone	25 CLINIC: Physical L.Asparaginase (Leg shot) Bactrim Dexamethasone.	26 Bactrim Dexamethasone	27 Ba De
31 **Happy Halloween** 👻 Dexamethasone	Bactrim: Pneumocystic, P Dexamethasone: Steroid Vincristine: chemother L-Asparaginase: Chem Counts: CBC/differen		

14

y	Thursday	Friday	Saturday
		1	2
	7	8	9
	14	15	16
ent (L Asp... ...) dcuo (leg stst) P)	21	22	23
e Dexamethasone	Dexamethasone	Dexamethasone	Dexamethasone
	28	29 CLINIC: ⏺our +c * Vi 3 ... (IVP) LAsp ... ... (Lu ... 6 T)	30
ic Dexamethasone prophalaxis) - 2 times a day Mon, Tues, and Wed - 2 times/day for 28 days sh) 2-3 out ug shot			

15

Sonnet for Queer Longing

We walk down St. Charles late one night after the parades.
Street sweepers are out, their open maws rake in go-cups,
beads, sludge. It's 4am and we are so very eighteen, wobbling
on cheap heels around potholes of green wetness.
You ask for my definition of love and I take a block to think.
We're still in it, cross-legged on the bed, barreling through yawn
after—my roommate's voice after saying, "You light up around
her." Thoughts accrue like weeds with oak tree
mothers who live centuries in one sustained embrace.
Endless green canopy, flowering thatched roof. I disappear
the weeds, invasive species that they are. Zephyrs roll
off the Mississippi, dead leaves ride the gust. My roommate drops
the subject. Next Mardi Gras I will drink less,
wear better shoes, walk home alone.

Interrogation

after Rebecca Tamás

How long have you been sick?

How.

Are you in remission?

A souped-up stasis between worlds.

Are you saying you've conjured other worlds? The otherworldly?

Careful with that word.

Have you taken part in banned ritual practices, medicinal or otherwise?

Blood.

What about blood?

BLOOD.

???

Bloodbloodbloodbloodbloodbloodblood badblood bloodblood

Ma'am, do you intend to cooperate? Haven't you caused enough trouble?

Trouble in the blood, trouble in the blood.

Do you always speak this way, in incantations?

Don't push your meaning on me, don't you do it.

Is that a threat?

The threat is in the blood.

You will not threaten me and get away with it.

I become a scarlet sash on your throat, rope of blood.

You have an unhealthy obsession with—

Rope of blood, rope of blood, rope of blood, rope, ROPE.

Olivia meets me at the coffee shop to give me her leftover Zoloft

her pills are much smaller / twenty-five milligrams to my hundred /
my pills could give birth / to hers / her pills the crumbs chiseled /
from my garish
marble rectangles / I wonder how much would be needed / to still a
wild boar /
I imagine the boar's face lulled quiet / placid as warm water / I take
the bottle
from her hand / shake it out of habit / tabs like dry baby teeth / I
think of downing
them all / all these teeth a fraction / of my daily dose / back to the
boar / we spoon
each other in a thicket / wild and out of sight / miles away / from
awake

I'll never forgive you for loving me most beautifully at the Super 8 in Lake Charles, LA

Thin sheets, analog clock radio, fatigued rattle
from the window unit. The shower rail you used
for leverage to enter my many rooms. Never
more animal, more feral or brute than inside
those yellowed walls. We took photos of ourselves
in a bed where many had fucked before us, would keep
fucking after us, ecstatic to capture desire in the face,
to prove to ourselves *this happened, we did this.*
The night cleaved in two like a peach & we patted each
other down, lingering in soft places. Puppy bellies stretched
under fluorescent lights. How come nothing was more tender
than the middle of the night when I had food poisoning & you
went into the strange dark for me? You took my pains as your own
in a room done up in cheap plaster that wouldn't last the summer.

You Followed Me to New York

On a day stubborn with rain
to a tiny room in Crown Heights
with a sink in the closet & an errant
mouse we named something I no
longer remember. What I do remember:
you arrived in Brooklyn on your birthday,
September, a light chill threaded the air.
You stepped out of a cab & my body
opened fully to you. My face lit like a bulb,
ecstatic as a baby who's found some
thing that moves her. Babies don't assign
names to things, & I admire them for it.
To name something is to punch a clock,
set it ticking toward a certain end. We
ducked into a cafe on Franklin Ave
to escape the rain, humidity turned sweat
on our foreheads. You were quiet, but you
were always quiet. Except today, I needed
your voice. I needed you to unstick your
thighs from the plastic chair, to meet my
gaze, hold it & say, "Erin." But you looked
down, at your phone, or out the window
at people wrestling with umbrellas, hidden
under scaffolds. You retrieved our coffee
from the counter, brought it back like
a funeral procession: slow, methodic,
focused. It was my turn to look out
the window, at the backdrop of our new
life. You said my name to break my gaze,

but the word fell from your mouth, rolled
on the floor. By the time it reached me,
it was a nothing-sound, meatless.
Could have been the rain.

Touch-Starved

Here I am:
hand in my pants on the hottest night
of the year, in an apartment with no central
air. This is how it goes. I feel hotter when
it's hot out, & summer with her long days
burns me like a pig on the spit. We
don't teach women how to touch
themselves, only others. Birds
have been using my fire escape
to fuck lately. Every time I look out
the window in daylight, there they are,
in the throes. I think they're mating wrens,
but I can't be bothered to look it up.
I am busy with the puzzle of my body,
the shape curled into a question mark.
The wrens are crowding me, loud in their
heat, each trill a demand: "Look!" I want
to tremble myself to pieces smaller
than dust. But if they're not fucking
they're trilling—not trilling then fucking.
Trill-fuck-trill. & the only cool spot in this
place is by the window. My fingers won't
soften enough to coax it, pluck it out
of its web, to draw that warm bloom.

Lagunitas

I go out for tampons, tea, and a cheap razor. Find them all at the new
bodega, the one with your name spelled the Spanish way—*Vicente.*
Then beers at your new place. I paint my mouth with a thick red brush.
A kindergartener trying at lips.

Railroad-style apartment, one half flooded with light. You live in the
dark half. Still, three rooms of your own in Brooklyn. It's not nothing.
"The room needs mood lighting," I say in each room. I drink four IPAs
even though I hate them. Little touches accumulate. A hand on the
hip, a finger on the neck. We hold vowels in our chests till they burst
from slack jaws. Is it overkill for a lover to arrive hungry? The onions
go *pap-pap* in the skillet. You clear the table of ashtrays and empties,
tell ex-girlfriend stories, proof you've been desired throughout history.
Low-hanging fruit.

I pretend to listen. Instead count your gray chest hairs, the years that
stretch between us. I fish my phone out of a pocket, the way anyone
does when they want to leave without leaving. Another round. You call
me your best friend, grab my face and kiss it. But a sentimental drunk
is still a drunk. You can't fall asleep without music, so you put something on. An important jazz ensemble I've never heard of, I'm sure.
Then a sudden, churning need for "air" after too many Lagunitas. My
steps thud down your stairs and out the door. I take the city's fickle
dark into my mouth as I walk, looking up into blue apartment windows, still hungry.

III

Glossary of Terms

after Franny Choi

	BLOOD	DARK	BED	MOUTH
Meaning	what lies beneath	lack and fullness	a resting place	a wellspring
See also	bone, lust, bile	pool, lay-ered blue	patch of soil	rivers, a child
Antonym	ghost	flame	drown	end
Origin	Germanic, to swell	Latin, as in a cave	Teutonic, to dig	Greek stóma, an opening
Dreams of being	what bursts out	a cloud	womb or mouth	womb or mouth

Alone / A Loan / All One

Knot of meat,
Fisted squirms.

Wall of cicada roar.
Wilted brood bent
back toward morning.

Nature, America,
group of hauntings,
valence of blood.

Ghosts linger between
each blade of grass.

I want to be wooed,
not wooden.

Tithes

Uncrash the car
Unyank the wheel
Uninduce speed
Untread   hundreds of miles
across state borders
Unlearn   *rush*   from the crunched metal
Unhex the heart of its   labors
Unclench: wheel

                        shoulders

                                    thighs

          breath.
Unsee roadside cattle   as dark   portents.
Unfold   darkly   from the driver's seat.
Untouch yourself   in your childhood   bed.
Untime,

               uncry,

                            unblood,
             call home.

I am Shakespeare's Woman

It hasn't always been this way:
blighted, leaking viscous fluids.

On a path of discovery, you make
wrong turns. Draw blood, unlearn hurt.

I want to see the sum total of parts,
see what lives inside red pock marks.

I have turned against my breasts.
Innocents, boulders shucked

from earthen tombs, brutalized.
Like peeling orange rinds until thumb

punctures flesh. Fingertips smudge blood
on my iPhone screen, brown my toothy nails.

I live by the blue light of your text replies.
Our bloods bleed blue until they oxidize.

Personal Injury

Something irredeemable about fist
fulls of cereal eaten over the sink.
Billboards for so many personal

injury lawyers visible from my window.
Dudley Debosier, Morris Bart, Gordon McKernan.
Call me NOW, Louisiana! Their eyes

glom on me across I-10, River Styx of the state.
Potholed, waterlogged everything. When
machine collides with body, it is personal.

When smoke coats my throat it's personal.
When nerves throttle my skin, when the storm
stretches my legs like a canvas when

rain paints my ugly blotches it is all
personal, and no one has run me my damages.
The lawyers stare but don't reply,

don't bother explaining why our state
leads the nation in profits gained
by selling us our own pain.

Ouroboros

One day I woke with wounds to the chest,
a creature slithered around my neck.
The snake devours the snake devours the rest.

It strikes if I struggle, part of the test.
I wait for it to sleep, but don't dare check.
One day I woke with wounds to the chest.

I dream of escape, become obsessed
with what all a snake can swallow whole.
The snake devours the snake devours the rest.

I shift its weight from my neck to my breasts.
Marbled eyes fly open—fangs fixed to hold.
Again I wake with wounds to the chest.

It speaks sometimes. It says I'm blessed
with another chance, *build us a home.*
The snake devours the snake devours the rest.

It reaches my mouth, makes me confess:
30 & alone, I can build a poem, not a home.
One day I woke with wounds to the chest.
The snake devours the snake devours the rest.

Take Notes on Everything

Half-light, but radiantly.
A pool is defined by
its limitations.
Loss of periphery,
loss of the side-body,
permanent upward gaze.
Furtive steps into morning
with jasmine on the breeze.
Mirror blues a ripple
on the surface,
how we communicate.
Not one damned cloud
in the way-up there.
Let the walls hug, let
them protect. Let
mother contain you
for now: without her
you'd be evaporated
into the jasmine bush.
Mother gives shape
to your wildness.
Thank her—
Mother potted you
so the only way to
grow is up.

Acknowledgments

I'm grateful to the literary magazines that published poems from this chapbook, sometimes in different forms: *Crab Creek Review*, *HAD*, *mutiny!*, *Prelude*, *The Shore*, *trampset*, and *Verse of April*.

The poem "Interrogation" was written after Rebecca Tamás's poem series of the same title from the 2019 book, *Witch*. The poem "Glossary of Terms" was written after Franny Choi's poem of the same title from the 2019 book, *Soft Science*.

My deep gratitude to the teachers and mentors whose wisdom in revision helped shape much of this chapbook, including John Biguenet, Mark Yakich, Alex Dimitrov, Shira Erlichman, Angel Nafis, Lara Glenum, and Brad Richard. To my best friend in poetry of the last decade, Andrew Ketcham, thank you for everything. Here's to another ten years writing together.

About the Author

Erin Little is a writer and editor from Dallas, Texas. After graduating with a B.A. in English from Loyola University New Orleans in 2015, she moved to New York to pursue a career in publishing. Over six years Erin worked as an editorial assistant for Columbia University Press, Routledge Research, and Penguin Random House. She will graduate with an MFA in creative writing from Louisiana State University in 2024. Her poems and essays have appeared in *Chestnut Review, Hobart After Dark, Juxtaprose Magazine, New Orleans Review, Prelude Magazine, The Shore*, and *trampset*. Find her online @little__erin.

Made in the USA
Las Vegas, NV
08 November 2023

80473427R00028